A FOREVER HOME FOR BELLA

Poppy's face softened. She crouched beside the eager puppy. "Hello, Bella," she murmured. Bella wagged her whole body, her little tail thwacking from side to side as Poppy rubbed her ears. "Do you remember me? Do you really?"

HAVE YOU READ?

A FOREVER HOME FOR **TILLY**

A FOREVER HOME FOR **PIP**

A FOREVER HOME FOR **LUNA**

A FOREVER HOME FOR **FLUFFY**

LOOK OUT FOR:

A FOREVER HOME FOR **TIGER**

A FOREVER HOME FOR
BELLA

LINDA CHAPMAN

Illustrated By
Sophy Williams

nosy
crow

First published in the UK in 2021 by Nosy Crow Ltd
The Crow's Nest, 14 Baden Place
Crosby Row, London SE1 1YW

www.nosycrow.com

ISBN: 978 1 78800 955 3

Nosy Crow and associated logos are trademarks and/or
registered trademarks of Nosy Crow Ltd.

Text copyright © Linda Chapman and Julie Sykes, 2021
Illustrations © Sophy Williams, 2021

The right of Linda Chapman, Julie Sykes and Sophy Williams
to be identified as the authors and illustrator respectively of this
work has been asserted by them in accordance with the Copyright,
Designs and Patents Act 1988.

A CIP catalogue record for this book will be available from the British Library.

Printed and bound in Great Britain by Clays Ltd, Elcograf S.p.A.

Papers used by Nosy Crow are made from
wood grown in sustainable forests.

MIX
Paper from
responsible sources
FSC® C018072

1 3 5 7 9 10 8 6 4 2

To Nathalie Fellows, Callie's favourite vet,
and to the real Bella and her little brother
Muzzy, two wonderful Labradors with
ever-wagging tails!

CHAPTER 1

Grace Taylor and her twin brother Jack were at the vet's for Tiny's annual check up. Despite his name, Tiny was a huge dog, with pointed ears, a very waggy tail and a thick white coat.

Grace gave Tiny a hug. "You've been

such a good boy," she told him, giggling as Tiny licked her face.

Nathalie, the vet, handed Tiny's vaccination card to Jack and gave Tiny a bone-shaped biscuit. "Tiny's in great condition. You two obviously look after him really well. But then I wouldn't expect anything less. How's Forever Homes going?"

Forever Homes was the twins' animal rehoming business. They took in cats and dogs whose owners couldn't keep them any more, and found them perfect new homes.

"We've rehomed two kittens," said Jack proudly. "Fluffy and Luna."

"And two puppies, Tilly and Pip," put in Grace. "They were super cute!"

"But we haven't got any animals in at the moment," said Jack. "I really wish we did."

"I'm sure another animal will come along soon," said Nathalie with a smile. "They usually seem to!"

The twins led Tiny back to the waiting room, where their mum gave him a hug. As she went to pay the bill, a woman with a yellow Labrador puppy burst through the front door. The puppy's tail wagged frantically. When it saw Tiny, it yapped and pulled to the end of its lead to say hello. The two dogs sniffed noses. The

puppy had dark eyes that sparkled with
mischief and fun. It was so cute, Grace just
wanted to scoop it up and cuddle it.

"Is it OK if I stroke your puppy?" Grace
asked the puppy's owner.

The woman nodded. "Of course. She's
called Bella. I'm Fliss."

Grace crouched down. "Hello, Bella."

The puppy jumped clumsily on to her lap. Grace giggled as she kissed the puppy's head. "She's gorgeous."

"Is she here for her vaccinations?" Jack asked, joining Grace.

"No, she had her last vaccination two weeks ago." Fliss swallowed. "The company I work for have just told me they're posting me abroad and I can't take Bella with me." Fliss looked at the puppy and her eyes filled with tears. "It's breaking my heart but I need to find Bella a new home as soon as possible. I came in because I remembered seeing a poster on the vet's notice board advertising a pet rehoming service."

"Maybe we can help," Grace said quickly. "We run Forever Homes, the

rehoming service. We put the poster up."

Together, the twins explained all about
Forever Homes.

"So you really think you could find Bella
a new home for me?" asked Fliss.

"Absolutely," said Jack. "We're experts.
And our mum runs a doggy daycare, so
she can help look after Bella too."

Mrs Taylor smiled and nodded. "I'm
sure Jack and Grace can help," she said.
"They make sure they find every animal
the right home."

The two grown-ups talked until
everything was agreed.

"I really don't want to say goodbye,"
said Fliss sadly. "But it will be tougher for
both of us if I keep her until I move, and it
won't be easy to pack with a lively puppy

    6

around who likes to chew things up!" She kissed Bella's head.

Bella wagged her tail so hard her bottom wiggled.

Grace gave Fliss a sympathetic look. "Please don't worry. We promise we'll take very good care of her."

Jack nodded. "We will. We'll find her an absolutely perfect new home!"

7

CHAPTER 2

Grace carried Bella out to the dogmobile, their mum's van. Their mum's doggy daycare business was called Top Dog, and her van was painted to look like a real dog. While Mum loaded Tiny into the back, Grace and Jack found a puppy seatbelt and

strapped Bella into the front seat between them.

Bella started to chew the seatbelt. Grace chuckled. "Bella, stop it!"

"Don't giggle. Say it like you mean it," said Jack.

Grace rolled her eyes at him but she knew that he was right. Bella would find it confusing if Grace laughed when she was telling her not to do something. "Leave," she said more strictly.

Bella stopped nibbling the seatbelt, "Good girl," said Grace. Bella looked at her for a second and then grabbed the ends of Grace's long hair and tried to chew them. "No, Bella!" Grace said, as she opened Bella's mouth and freed her hair. "No chewing."

When they arrived back to their old, rambling house, they took Bella through the yard and into the garden. The shed they used for their office was at the bottom. Grace, who loved to paint, had made the Forever Homes sign that hung on the door. It was cosy inside, with a stripy rug on the floor, a comfy chair and a desk with another chair. Grace had stuck some of her drawings on the walls and there was also a large pinboard covered with photographs of all the animals they had helped. There were boxes of dog and cat toys on the floor and several large jars full of treats.

"Welcome to Forever Homes, Bella," said Grace, putting the puppy down on the floor. While Jack sat at the desk and

   10

wrote Bella's details in their special blue
notebook, Bella trotted around the room,
her tail wagging non-stop as she explored
her new surroundings.

Bella spotted the crate of dog
toys. She stuck her nose
inside and picked
up a squeaky
rubber
bone. She
chewed
it for a
moment
and then lost interest.

Going back to the desk, she put her paws
on Jack's legs. Jack lifted her on to his
lap and immediately Bella nibbled at the
notebook.

11

"No," Jack said.

Bella stopped and looked at him with her head on one side. "This is for writing in, Bella," Jack told her, "not chewing." Bella watched as he made some notes. "She seems like a fast learner and very inquisitive," Jack said to Grace. He put Bella back on the ground. "Try some of our tests."

The twins always tried out personality tests on the animals they were rehoming. It helped them to match each puppy or kitten with their perfect owner.

Grace took a ball on a rope from the crate of toys and rolled it across the floor. Bella bounded after it and brought it back to Grace, her tail wagging. "She's good at retrieving," said Jack, noting it down.

"Good girl," Grace praised Bella, giving her a treat in exchange for the ball. Bella gobbled it up and then nudged Grace's hands hopefully.

"I think she's going to be quite greedy," said Grace. "Write that down, and also that she's very friendly," she added, giggling as Bella jumped on to her lap and licked her face.

"Full of energy," noted Jack as Bella bounded away again. "She'll need an owner who can give her lots of exercise."

Bella had gone to the toy crate again. This time she pulled out a paperback book.

"That's mine! I wondered where it had got to," said Grace. Bella trotted around the shed, looking very proud of her find. Plonking herself down in one corner, she started to chew the spine. "No!" said Grace, hastily taking the book away. "That's naughty."

Bella rolled over on to her side, showing her pink tummy. Grace smiled. This was the puppy's way of asking not to be told off any more. "OK, I forgive you. You're probably teething at the moment, so you like to chew things, but no more chewing books."

Jack came over to join them. "I've written that she likes books ... for dinner."

Grace smiled. "She is cheeky, but so sweet. We'll find a home for her soon, I know we will."

Jack nodded. "But only the perfect home will do!"

"Has anyone seen my drumsticks?" said Ollie, the twins' seventeen-year-old brother, later that night. They were all sitting in the lounge after dinner.

"Nope," said Amelia, the twins' thirteen-year-old sister, barely looking up from her phone.

Bella peered out from behind the sofa. She was holding a drumstick in her mouth and her tail was wagging hard.

Grace put down her book and pulled a dog treat out of her pocket. "Here, Bella!" Bella trotted over and dropped the drumstick. Grace handed it back to Ollie.

"It's got teeth marks in," Ollie complained.

"You shouldn't have left it lying around then," said Jack. "We did warn you that Bella chews."

"With any luck, the teeth marks will make you play better," said Grace grinning.

"She's so cute." Ollie stroked Bella's head and she tried to bite his hand.

"No, Bella!" scolded Grace. "Settle down and I'll play with you when I've finished this chapter." Grace picked up her book again. Bella climbed on to her lap and

nibbled the edge of the page. Grace held it out of her way, reading the words aloud, hoping it would calm her. Gradually Bella stopped struggling and snuggled down in Grace's lap with her brown eyes fixed on Grace's face.

"Jack, look," whispered Grace, pausing. "Bella's listening to the story."

"Dogs can't understand stories," said Jack. But as Grace continued reading, he

became less sure. Bella really did seem to be listening. She tensed as the story got more exciting then relaxed when the children in it managed to save themselves from danger.

Grace grinned. "Maybe we should find a librarian to rehome her with!"

She was joking but Jack looked thoughtful. "That's not a bad idea," he said. "Why don't we call into the town library tomorrow after school?"

Bella started to chew Grace's book again. Grace whisked it out of her reach. "OK! But no more chewing books, Bella. They're just for reading. Understand?"

Bella gave her a cheeky look and thumped her tail in reply.

CHAPTER 3

At school the following day the twins'
teacher, Ms Drew, took the class to the
school library. "We are starting a new
science topic called 'Living Things'. You
should each choose a partner for a project
on baby animals."

Baby animals, thought Grace. *Brilliant!*

Ms Drew handed out large pieces of card. "Each pair must research a particular animal baby and record their findings on a poster. You can use the books and the computers."

Grace caught the eye of her friend Poppy Hyder. They weren't usually allowed to sit together because they could never help chatting and giggling. Grace silently mouthed "Partners?" to her, and Poppy smiled and nodded enthusiastically.

When Ms Drew had finished explaining the project, Grace and Poppy walked over to the bookshelves and sat down. "This is going to be so much fun," said Grace.

"Yes, I've got loads of animal books at home," said Poppy. "Baby animals

are really cute, much cuter than baby humans."

"How's your baby sister?" Grace asked. Poppy's mum had had a baby a month ago.

Poppy pulled a face. "Boring. All she does is drink milk and burp."

Grace giggled. "Bella, the new puppy that we're trying to rehome, does tiny burps after she's eaten. I think it sounds really sweet."

"I wish we had a puppy instead of Rose. There is nothing sweet about her," said Poppy. "She burped during Sunday lunch and was sick all down Mum's T-shirt. It was gross but Granny laughed and clapped like Rose had done something amazing! Grandad gave her this weird goofy look and said, 'That girl is going to go far.'"

Poppy sighed. "I told him that Rose could definitely win a gold medal for burping at the next Olympics, but Granny said I was being silly. Then Mum sent me to the kitchen to get the pudding."

Grace burst out laughing. "I'd love to see an Olympic burping competition."

"Me too," said Poppy, but then she frowned. "I thought it would be fun having a baby sister but it's not. Mum and Dad are so busy with her, they hardly seem to notice me any more. Mum even forgot to pick me up from running club last week. The coach had to phone her to remind her to come and get me."

Grace didn't know what to say. Poppy was usually so cheerful and funny, nothing ever seemed to bother her, but now she

was looking miserable. She thought for a moment and then nudged her. "Hey, Pops, how does a baby tell its mum it needs a nappy change?"

Poppy frowned. "How?"

"It sends its mum a *pee-mail*!"

Both girls burst out laughing.

Ms Drew came over. "Have you decided on your topic, girls? Where are the books you're going to use?"

Poppy sent Grace an alarmed look.

      23

"We ... um ... we don't need books, miss!" Grace invented quickly. "We're going to do a project on the new Labrador puppy that Jack and I are looking after."

"Oh," said Ms Drew.

"She's called Bella and she's really cute," Grace continued. "We'll be able to write loads about her."

"Our project is going to be the best!" Poppy chimed in.

"Could I bring her into school one day?" Grace asked Ms Drew hopefully. "Then everyone can see a real baby animal."

"That's a great plan, Grace," said Ms Drew. "I'll have a chat with your mum about it first to check that it's OK. Well done, girls." She smiled at them and walked on.

   24

Grace and Poppy breathed out sighs of relief. "That was a brilliant idea!" Poppy whispered.

"Why don't you ask your mum to bring Rose in and the class could see a human baby too?" suggested Grace.

Poppy pulled a face. "No way! It's bad enough putting up with Rose at home. I don't want her in school." She jumped to her feet. "Let's go back to the classroom and start on our poster. You can draw some cartoon dogs around the border and then we can write some facts in boxes." She hurried off, tickling their friend Chloe as she passed and making her squeal.

Grace followed her more slowly. Poppy had looked so unhappy when she talked about her baby sister. *She's been an only*

child for so long, it must be weird sharing her mum and dad now, Grace thought, watching her friend. She wished there was something she could do to help Poppy. But what?

CHAPTER 4

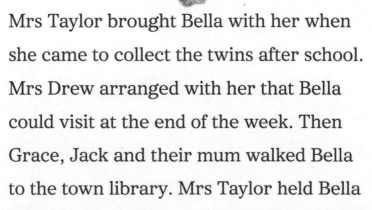

Mrs Taylor brought Bella with her when
she came to collect the twins after school.
Mrs Drew arranged with her that Bella
could visit at the end of the week. Then
Grace, Jack and their mum walked Bella
to the town library. Mrs Taylor held Bella

while the twins went inside to talk to the librarians, as only trained assistance dogs were allowed inside.

"I'd love a Labrador puppy," said Margaret, one of the librarians, when the twins explained why they were there. "My grandchildren would like a dog too and they'd help walk her. I only work part-time so maybe I could take your puppy on."

"Can you come outside and see her?" said Grace, exchanging hopeful looks with Jack.

"You can bring her inside for a few minutes," said Jayne, the chief librarian. "It's not too busy at the moment and I'd love a quick cuddle with a puppy!"

The twins fetched Bella. She looked

around inquisitively with her ears pricked
and greeted the librarians with tail wags.

"She's so sweet," said Margaret, putting
a pile of books down on the floor. "Would
you like to come and live with me then,
Bella?"

Bella licked her hand then sniffed at
the pile of books. She started to chew
the corners. "Oh, no!" Margaret gasped,
pulling the books out of Bella's reach.

"Sorry, Bella's teething at the moment
so she often chews things," said Jack.

"She could be trained not to though,"
said Mrs Taylor.

Margaret shook her head. "I'm sorry
but my house is full of books and they're
all really precious to me. What if Bella
damaged some of them while she was

being trained? She's lovely but I think I need an older dog who's past the chewing stage."

Jack sighed. "Yes, that probably would be better."

When everyone had finished cuddling Bella, the twins and their mum walked her home.

"None of the librarians will give Bella a home then," said Jack.

"Nope, we'd better keep searching," agreed Grace sadly.

On the morning of Bella's visit to school, Grace and Jack brushed her coat until it shone. As Bella trotted into the playground with them the children crowded round, all wanting to pat her.

"Please can you all stand back a bit?"
said Jack. Bella didn't look worried at all
but he was concerned that someone was
going to stand on one of her paws.

    31

"Come on, everyone, you heard Jack. Move back!" ordered Poppy, marching over, clapping her hands and shooing people away.

Grace shot her a grateful look. Poppy was sometimes a bit too bossy but right now it was good to have her there to organise things.

"You're still too close!" Poppy told some Year Fours. "Stand back, please."

Everyone shuffled aside and Grace led Bella through the gap Poppy had created. Poppy followed them into school. "I'm doing a project on Bella. I'm allowed to go in too!" she said importantly before shutting the door behind them.

"Thanks, Poppy!" said Grace.

Poppy crouched down. "Aren't you the

cutest puppy ever!" she said, grinning as Bella climbed on her knee and licked her face. "And you have a very tickly tongue!" Bella started to pant. Poppy looked concerned. "Are you thirsty, Bella?" She looked at the twins. "Shall I go and get her some water?"

"That would be great," said Jack. "Thanks."

Poppy hurried off and came back with a plastic bowl filled with water. She put it down and Bella lapped it up. Poppy grinned. "OK, you two wait here and get her settled and I'll go and find Ms Drew."

Jack raised his eyebrows as Poppy left. "Poppy is so bossy!"

"She can be but she's very good with Bella," said Grace.

Jack gave her a thoughtful look. "Could she be a possible owner?"

Grace shook her head. "I don't think so. Her mum's just had a baby. They're not going to want a puppy as well."

"I guess not," said Jack.

Just then Poppy appeared with Ms Drew and Ms Clark, the headteacher.

"I had to come and see this beautiful puppy," Ms Clark said with a smile, crouching down to say hello to Bella. "I love Labs."

Bella wagged her whole body in greeting. "Well, aren't you a friendly little girl?" said Ms Clark.

Grace gave the headteacher a hopeful look. "Would you like a puppy, Ms Clark?"

"If you're interested we could come and do a home check," said Jack.

"I would love to have Bella," said Ms Clark. "My husband and I are keen walkers and we really want a dog to take walking with us but we're out of the house all day in term-time and some evenings too. That's not ideal for a puppy."

Grace and Jack sighed. It really wasn't ideal.

"It's a pity people can't have part-time dogs," Ms Clark went on with a smile. "Then I'd definitely have her. Oh well, much as I'd love to stay here and cuddle Bella, I'd better get on!"

After she'd left, the twins and Poppy settled Bella in the reading corner. Then everyone else came in from the playground.

After Ms Drew had taken the register she asked the twins to tell the class about their puppy.

"We've had Bella for almost a week now. She's fourteen weeks old," Jack began. "She started eating solid food at three

 36

weeks old. Before that she just drank milk. She left her mum when she was eight weeks old. She's very clever and she's already learned the basic commands like sit, stay and lie down. She also tells us when she wants to go to the toilet by sitting at the door and whining."

"Puppies aren't allowed to walk in public spaces until they've been vaccinated because they might pick up dangerous doggy illnesses like parvovirus," Grace chipped in. "But Bella's up to date with her vaccinations and she's allowed to go out now."

"Can we stroke her?" asked Chloe eagerly.

Ms Drew went round the circle of children so that everyone could stroke

Bella. Janie, who was sitting next to Poppy, squealed when Bella tried to nibble her fingers. She pulled her hands away quickly and shuffled back. Bella bounced after her and Janie shrieked, "She's going to bite me!"

"Don't be silly!" Poppy said as Bella stopped, looking confused. "She's not

going to bite you. She thinks you want
to play because you're jumping around.
Here, Bella." She tapped her hand on the
floor. Bella trotted over. She lay down
and tried to nibble Poppy's fingers. "No,"
Poppy said firmly, and gently rolled Bella
on to her back, tickling her tummy to
distract her.

Ms Drew looked impressed. "You're a natural, Poppy."

"I really wish I could have a dog," Poppy said longingly.

Grace and Jack looked at each other and Grace was sure they were having the same thought. Should they ask Poppy if she could give Bella a home? Maybe her parents would say yes despite the baby.

When everyone had fussed Bella, Ms Drew told them some more facts about puppies. Then it was time for Jack and Grace to take Bella to the reception area where their mum was meeting them to take the puppy home.

Once the twins were out of the classroom, they faced each other excitedly. "You were thinking that we should ask Poppy if she can give Bella a home?" Grace said.

Jack nodded. "She'd have to pass our home checks first but she could be perfect. She does a lot of running – Bella could go out with her when she's old enough. Poppy's also patient but firm. I'm sure she'd train Bella well."

"Their house has a nice big garden that's fenced, and Labradors are usually good family dogs so Bella should be fine with the baby. Let's ask her at break time!" Grace said eagerly.

They reached the school's reception area. Their mum hadn't arrived so they waited near the door. Mr Wong, a retired teacher, was sitting on a sofa, listening to a Year Two girl reading. She had her back to the twins. Glancing at them, Mr Wong put his finger to his lips so they knew they should be quiet.

"The cat and the fox made a w ... w..." The girl struggled with a word and then shook her head. "I can't do it."

"Yes, you can, Sienna," Mr Wong encouraged. "Try to sound the word out."

"W... I..." Sienna shook her head. "No, I can't." She gave a little gasp as Bella pushed her way round the sofa and looked up at her. "It's a puppy!" she said in surprise.

"Sorry!" said Grace hastily, tightening the lead. "Our mum's coming to pick her up. We brought her in because our class is doing a project on baby animals."

"She's beautiful," said Sienna, stroking Bella.

"I think she was enjoying your story," said Jack with a smile, as Bella nudged the book with her nose.

"Can I read to her?" said Sienna, looking at Mr Wong.

He nodded. "If you like."

With one hand stroking Bella, Sienna slowly read out the sentence she'd been struggling with: "The cat and the fox made a wish. They wished that they could go on holi ... holiday to the beach."

She kept reading. Bella lay down and

listened, her head on one side. Having her there seemed to encourage Sienna. By the time Mrs Taylor arrived she had read six whole pages and shown Bella all the pictures.

"Sorry I'm late!" said the twins' mum. "I hope Bella's not being a nuisance."

"Not at all. In fact, she's been a great help," said Mr Wong, smiling.

"I've never read so much in one go before, have I, Mr Wong?" said Sienna. "Can Bella come back another day?"

"We'll see," said Mrs Taylor. She scooped up the sleepy puppy. "It looks like she's ready for a rest now."

Jack and Grace waved their mum off and went back to class.

Grace sat down next to Poppy.

"I wish Bella was still here!" Poppy said.

Grace remembered what she and Jack had been talking about and the words spilled out of her. "Would you like to be Bella's new owner? Jack and I think you'd be perfect."

"Me? Wow! I'd love to!" gasped Poppy. "Mum and Dad promised to let me have a dog when I'm twelve but maybe they'll let me have one early. Mum's given up work now she's had Rose so there's someone home each day and I'm definitely old enough to look after her." Her eyes shone. "I'll ask them tonight!" She grabbed Grace's hands, her eyes shining. "Fingers crossed they say yes!"

CHAPTER 5

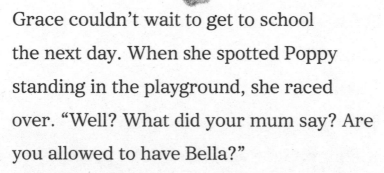

Grace couldn't wait to get to school
the next day. When she spotted Poppy
standing in the playground, she raced
over. "Well? What did your mum say? Are
you allowed to have Bella?"

"No." Poppy scowled and kicked a stone.

"Mum said she already had enough to do with me and Rose. It's not true. She hardly does anything for me since Rose arrived."

Grace's heart sank. "I guess babies do need a lot of attention when they're tiny," she said. "I'm sure your mum loves you and Rose just the same."

Ramming her hands in her pockets, Poppy said fiercely, "Then why does Rose always come first? Mum said instead of a puppy I could have an extra session at running club. But I don't want that, I want Bella." She folded her arms. Her eyes looked bright, as if she was about to cry.

Grace felt awful. "I'm sorry. I guess at least you get extra running time."

Poppy's face darkened. "She probably only agreed to that so she can have more

   48

time alone with perfect little Rose!" She stomped off.

Jack came over. "No luck?"

"No," Grace sighed. "Her mum said no."

"We'd better keep looking for a home then," said Jack.

Grace nodded sadly. "But Poppy would have been just right for Bella."

"Don't worry," Jack comforted her. "A new owner is sure to come along soon."

"Mmm," said Grace. "I guess so. Or maybe we could persuade Ms Clark to work part-time—"

"Wait!" Jack interrupted.

His eyes had lit up like they always did when he had an awesome idea.

"What?" Grace demanded.

"I might have thought of something," said Jack mysteriously. "I'll need to check though."

Just then one of the teachers came out and rang the bell. Jack hurried to line up.

Grace went after him. "What's your idea?"

Jack tapped his nose. "Nope, you'll have to wait! But I might have a brilliant way to let both Ms Clark *and* Poppy have Bella – and for us to be able to see her too!"

That morning Jack and Grace's class were working on their baby animal projects. Grace finished the border of cartoon dogs on the poster she and Poppy were making together. Poppy started off writing some puppy facts down but she quickly got bored and started looking up puppy jokes on the Internet instead.

"Hey, Grace! Here's one. What do you call a snowman's dog? A slush puppy!" Poppy giggled and nudged Grace. "That's a good one, isn't it? Maybe we should have a joke section on our poster?"

   51

Grace laughed but then she noticed Ms Drew looking at them. "We need to write some facts down or we'll get into trouble," she said.

While Poppy found more animal jokes, Grace started to write down facts about puppies. After a while she looked round and noticed that Jack was reading something on one of the computers. She could tell he was excited from the look on

his face. She watched as he made some notes. What was he up to?

"OK, tell me your idea or I'm going to burst!" she said at break time, running over to him.

Jack opened his notebook. There was a page of notes and at the top he'd written in big letters: SCHOOL DOG!

Grace stared.

"School dogs!" said Jack eagerly, waving the notebook at her. "Yesterday when I was looking up stuff for the animal project, I read something about schools that have dogs. They go and live with teachers, like Ms Clark, after school and in the evenings and holidays. A dog in school is supposed to be really good for pupils with anxiety or home issues. Well, couldn't Bella be a school dog?" He looked really excited. "She's so friendly and she had a great time here yesterday—"

"Yes!" broke in Grace. "And she loved it when Sienna read to her. All the little ones could practise by reading to her. And Poppy would be able to see her loads. It's the best idea you've ever had, Jack!"

Jack looked pleased. "If Ms Clark agrees she really could have a part-time dog!"

"Let's go and ask her right now!" cried Grace.

CHAPTER 6

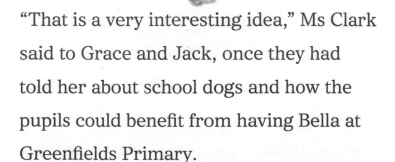

"That is a very interesting idea," Ms Clark said to Grace and Jack, once they had told her about school dogs and how the pupils could benefit from having Bella at Greenfields Primary.

"Bella would have to live with a member

of staff when she wasn't in school," said Grace. "So you could be Bella's new owner after all."

Ms Clark looked thoughtful. "This might actually work. Thank you both. I'll do some research and let you know as soon as I can."

Grace couldn't help feeling disappointed as they walked back to class. "Why didn't she just say yes?"

"I suppose she needs to talk to the other teachers," said Jack sensibly.

"I guess," said Grace. "I can't wait to tell Poppy. She's going to love the idea!"

However, when she told Poppy that they were hoping that Bella could become a school dog, Poppy scowled. "It's a rubbish idea. Bella would hate being a school dog.

She needs one special person to love her, not a whole school."

Grace's mouth fell open. "I don't understand. I thought you'd be pleased. If Bella comes here you still get to see her."

Poppy's frown deepened. "I'm already sharing my mum and dad. I don't want to share a dog too!" she snapped.

"But that's just—" Grace had been about to say *stupid* but Jack saw the unhappiness on Poppy's face and jumped in.

"We're sorry, Poppy. We didn't mean to upset you," he said.

"I want Bella to be mine!" Poppy burst out and, blinking back tears, she turned and ran away.

"Oh dear, that didn't go well," sighed Jack.

Grace nodded, feeling torn. She felt sorry for Poppy but still wanted their plan for Bella to go ahead. "I hope Poppy gets used to the idea," she said slowly.

"And that Ms Clark says yes," added Jack.

A few days later Ms Clark called Grace and Jack into her office. Standing in front of the headteacher's desk, Grace hopped nervously from one foot to the other. This had to be about Bella. What had Ms Clark decided?

"Well..." A smile broke out on Ms Clark's face. "After looking into the matter and discussing it with the teachers and the governors, I have decided I would love to rehome Bella and to have her as a school dog, if that's still OK with both of you?"

Grace felt like hugging her

headteacher.

"Yes, it is!"

she cried.

She tried not

to think about

how Poppy

would react.

Jack's eyes

shone with

happiness.

"Normally

we'd do

a home

check," he said.

"You're more than welcome to come

round to my house," said Ms Clark.

Grace looked at Jack. It would be really weird going to inspect their headteacher's house! But he nodded at Ms Clark.

"Thanks. We could come this evening about six? Mum or Dad could bring us round, or Ollie, our big brother, could if they're busy."

"Oliver Taylor," Ms Clark mused. "I remember he was always breaking his pencils pretending to play the drums on the table. I'll phone your parents and let them know what's happening. In the meantime, could you think about what we need in school to make it safe for Bella? I'll have to do a formal risk assessment, but any ideas you have will help."

The twins spent their lunchtime making a list of the things Bella would need, like

dog beds and bowls, and the best place to put them so that Bella could have her own safe space. Jack also added to the list covers for plug sockets and two stair gates for the doors – particularly the one into the library so Bella couldn't chew the books!

"Bella's personality test shows that she's inquisitive so we must make sure everywhere is safe." Jack consulted his notebook. "She's also energetic and needs exercise so we could ask Ms Drew to appoint a dog monitor, someone to take Bella outside regularly and to help train her."

"Poppy would be a perfect school-dog carer if she'd do it," said Grace.

"Do you think she would?" said Jack.

Grace looked determined. "I'm sure we could persuade her," she said. "But first Ms Clark needs to pass our home check!"

At six o'clock Ollie drove Grace, Jack and Bella round to Ms Clark's house. "I'll wait here," he said getting out his phone. "I'm not going in."

"Ms Clark's nice," said Jack.

"She's my old headteacher!" said Ollie, looking at him as if he was crazy.

Grace took Bella out of the travel crate in the back of the car and Jack rang the doorbell. A tall man with a friendly smile answered.

"I'm Martin Clark. You must be Grace and Jack and this must be Bella. Come along in," he said, standing back as the

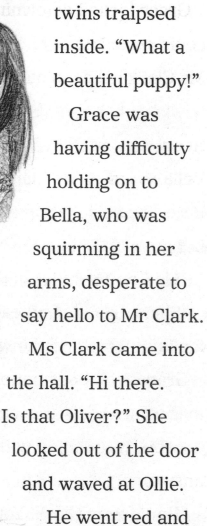

twins traipsed inside. "What a beautiful puppy!" Grace was having difficulty holding on to Bella, who was squirming in her arms, desperate to say hello to Mr Clark. Ms Clark came into the hall. "Hi there. Is that Oliver?" She looked out of the door and waved at Ollie.

He went red and pretended not to see her.

Grace grinned and put Bella down as Ms

Clark shut the door. The puppy charged along the hall. They all followed her into the kitchen, a large tiled room with a breakfast bar and glass doors that opened on to a fenced garden.

"This is perfect," said Jack, looking out of the window. "There's plenty of room for Bella to safely run around outside."

Grace nodded, her eyes widening as she noticed a box of chocolate puffs on the worktop. *Ms Clark eats chocolate puffs!* She giggled.

Jack shot her a stern look. Grace hid her laugh by pretending to cough.

"Bella will sleep in here." Ms Clark opened a door to a smaller room with a sink and a washing machine.

Bella rushed past Grace and ran to a

basket full of washing on the floor. Sticking her nose inside, she pulled something out.

"Bella, no. Drop!" gasped Grace.

Wagging her tail, Bella rushed back into the kitchen carrying a sock.

"She still needs some training," said Jack hurriedly.

Grace caught up with the puppy. "Drop," she said firmly, as she gently began to prise the sock from Bella's mouth.

Reluctantly Bella let go and the soggy pink sock decorated with unicorns and stars fell on the floor. Grace felt more laughter bubbling up inside her. Ms Clark also liked unicorns!

"Good girl," Grace praised Bella, feeding her a dog treat from her pocket.

As Bella crunched on the treat, Ms Clark rescued the sock.

"I'll get Bella some special chew toys while she's getting her adult teeth," she said. "It'll be fun having a puppy around the house, and when she's old enough we'll take her for lots of long walks. Martin and I are sometimes both out in the evenings and we do go abroad in the holidays but I'm sure I can find a puppy-sitter."

"That all sounds great," said Jack. "Your house is perfect." He looked at Grace and she nodded in agreement. "We're pleased to tell you that it's passed the Forever Homes inspection. As soon as the school has been puppy-proofed, Bella can become the school dog and move in with you. I made some notes about everything that needs doing." He had typed the list up when he got home and now handed the notes to Ms Clark.

"This is great. Thanks, Jack," she said.

"There was one more thing," said Grace. "We thought there should be a dog monitor or carer who makes sure that Bella gets exercised and trained while she's at school."

"And also makes sure she has time to

 68

sleep and doesn't get overtired," said Jack.

Ms Clark's eyes twinkled. "I expect that you two would like that job?"

"We would," said Grace. "But it might be nice for someone else to look after Bella, someone who doesn't have a dog of their own..."

"Someone who really wants one," put in Jack. "Like Poppy in our class. Could she be Bella's carer instead of us?"

Ms Clark nodded. "That's a great idea. I'll ask her in the morning."

Grace remembered the way Poppy had reacted when they had first told her their idea and she crossed her fingers.

Oh, I hope Poppy says yes, she thought.

CHAPTER 7

Although Bella wasn't going to start at
school until it was fully puppy-proofed, the
next day the twins' mum said they could
walk her to school.

"The more she gets used to the place
and all the children the better," said Mrs

Taylor. "I'll walk her back afterwards."

As they went into the playground, Grace spotted Poppy. "Here, take Bella," she said, handing Jack Bella's lead. She ran over. "Hi, Poppy," she called.

"Hi," said Poppy.

Grace took a breath. "Poppy, I've got something to ask you. Ms Clark said Bella can be a school dog but she needs someone to be responsible for her. A dog monitor who would help to look after and train her while she's at school." She saw Poppy start to shake her head and rushed on. "Ms Clark is going to ask you. Please say yes."

"No, I don't want to," Poppy said tightly.

"You'd be brilliant at it!" said Grace, refusing to give up. She waved at Jack. To

   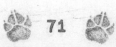

her relief, he understood and brought Bella over. Seeing Poppy, the puppy gave a woof of delight and jumped up at her. "See, she remembers you," said Grace as Bella's pink tongue licked at Poppy's hands.

"She hasn't greeted anyone else like that," said Jack.

"She'd really like you to be her school carer," said Grace.

Poppy's face softened. She crouched beside the eager puppy. "Hello, Bella," she murmured. Bella wagged her whole body, her little tail thwacking from side to side as Poppy rubbed her ears. "Do you remember me? Do you really?"

Bella stuck her nose in Poppy's face and snuffled at her hair.

"That's a yes!" said Grace.

Poppy laughed. "Would you like me to look after you?" Bella licked Poppy's face and cuddled closer.

"There'll be lots to do. You'll have to take her out, make sure she has water, give her lunch and make sure she has rest times. You'll also have to train her and supervise the little ones with her," said Jack.

"It would be almost like she was your dog," added Grace. "It's a big responsibility but you'd be the best person in the school to do it."

"Will you?" asked Jack.

Poppy's face broke into a delighted smile. "Yes!" she said, kissing Bella's head. "All right, I will!"

Two months later Bella had settled into

her role as Greenfields' school dog and
Poppy was a brilliant school-dog carer.
She was confident, and great at training
Bella and the younger children! She'd even
started a Puppy Club where she taught
them how to look after Bella. And her
parents agreed that Bella could come

to their house on the
evenings when
Ms Clark and
her husband
were out.

"Bella loves Puppy Club," Poppy told Grace and Jack at the end of school one day. Bella was on a lead because she was going to Poppy's house for the evening. "I always finish by reading a dog story. Bella sits on the beanbag with me. She likes the funny books best. When everyone laughs she opens her mouth as if she's joining in. I've finally taught her to love books by listening to them rather than nibbling them!" Bella thumped her tail as if she agreed.

Grace laughed. "She is a very clever dog," she said, patting her.

Poppy grinned. "She really is."

A little boy called Ethan came running up with a couple of friends. "Bella's the best dog in the world!" He dropped down

and threw his arms round her.

"Be careful, Ethan," said Poppy. "Don't hold her too tightly. She likes it better if you stroke her gently just like I showed you in Puppy Club, remember?"

Ethan released his grip and Poppy guided his hand so he was stroking Bella's back in the direction of her fur. "That's it, like that. See, she's wagging her tail. You're making her happy!"

"Can we stroke her too?" asked one of the girls who was with Ethan.

Grace and Jack watched as Poppy patiently let the three younger children all stroke Bella. "OK, that's enough now,' she said. "You can cuddle her some more tomorrow." She grinned at Jack and Grace. "It's hard managing Bella's fan club!"

"You're brilliant at it though," said Jack.

"I thought I didn't like little kids," said Poppy. "But it's been fun teaching them about Bella. I think that when Rose gets bigger it might not be so bad having a little sister after all. I can show her how to look after Bella too. Mum and Dad are really proud of me for looking after Bella so well and they said we can have a family dog when Rose is a bit older." She crouched down and fussed Bella, who licked her face. "I'd rather have you part-time than have any other dog though. You're the best!" Bella licked her face and woofed.

"I think she agrees!" said Jack.

"Looking after Bella's made me realise how much work a puppy is," Poppy said. "It's the same with babies. I can see why

Mum needs to spend so much time with Rose now and why she gets so tired. Bella's already much easier to look after, and hopefully Rose will be too." She waved

as she spotted her mum and Rose. "There they are! See you tomorrow!"

She ran off with Bella bounding at her side. "Hi, Mum! Hello, Rosie Posy."

Poppy lifted Bella up to the pram for Rose to see her. "Say hello to Bella!" She gently waved Bella's paw and Rose giggled.

Grace looked at Jack, her eyes shining. "We did it!" she said. "We found Bella a perfect home."

"Not just one perfect home but two," said Jack. "And we made both Poppy and Ms Clark really happy."

"I wonder what's next," said Grace thoughtfully. "How about a school cat? If our next animal in need of a home is a kitten."

Jack nodded. "Why not? We could have a school cat, a school rabbit, a school pony..."

"A school giraffe!" Grace put in, grinning.

"Maybe even a school elephant!" said
Jack. "The more animals the better!"

Grace met his hand in a high-five.
"Definitely!" she agreed.

TINY'S FACT FILE

NAME: Tiny

AGE: Six

BREED: German Shepherd crossbreed

COLOUR: White

SIZE: Very big

LIKES: Being cuddled, going on walks, sitting on people's feet so they can't move away, making friends with other animals, and, of course, Grace and Jack!

DISLIKES: Baths

FAVOURITE TREATS: Sausages and cheese

WHICH DOG IS PERFECT FOR YOU?

Answer these questions to find out if your ideal dog is a Jack Russell terrier, a Springer Spaniel, a Labrador Retriever or a German Shepherd!

1. **WHICH OF THE FOLLOWING DESCRIPTIONS IS MOST LIKE YOU:**
    a) I love running around and playing games with my friends
    b) I'm good at sports and I like to win! I don't always do what I'm told...
    c) I like making friends and I'm

   84

good at making people happy

d) I'm clever and good at solving
   problems. I can be a bit stubborn!

2. **WHAT ARE YOUR FAVOURITE THINGS IN LIFE?**

   a) Running, jumping, chasing
      and playing!
   b) Making a lot of noise
   c) Eating delicious food
   d) Being with my best friend

3. **WHAT WOULD BE YOUR PERFECT DAY?**

    a) A fun walk in the countryside, followed by a run!

    b) Football, basketball and having play fights with my friends

    c) Playing outside all morning, a big lunch, then a cosy afternoon indoors

    d) A long walk on the beach with my best friend

YOUR IDEAL DOG IS A...

Mainly a) A fun Springer Spaniel! They never seem to get tired no matter how much exercise they have and the second you move, so do they!

Mainly b) A lively Jack Russell terrier! They love to chase, bark and play fight and are great fun to be with, although they don't always do what they're told!

Mainly c) An easy-going Labrador Retriever. They love to fetch and like to please. They are friendly and get on with everyone, and they love food!

Mainly d) A faithful German Shepherd. They are one of the most intelligent dog breeds. Their brains need to be active, they love to work and are very loyal to their owners.

LABRADORS ARE LOVELY! DID YOU KNOW THAT:

- Labradors can be either black, brown (chocolate) or yellow (golden). You can get all three colours in one litter of puppies!
- Labradors originated in Newfoundland in Canada.
- Labradors are bred to retrieve and love to carry things around in their mouths. They should have "soft" mouths which means they carry things gently – some Labradors can even carry an egg without breaking it!
- Labradors are great swimmers and usually love water.

GRACE AND JACK'S FAVOURITE DOGGIE JOKES

WHICH DOG BREED ABSOLUTELY LOVES LIVING IN THE CITY?

A New Yorkie!

WHAT DO YOU GET WHEN YOU CROSS A COCKER SPANIEL, A POODLE, AND A ROOSTER?

A Cockerpoodledoo!

WHAT DO YOU GET WHEN YOU CROSS A DOG WITH A PHONE?

A Golden Receiver!